April Galleons

ALSO BY JOHN ASHBERY

POETRY

Some Trees
The Tennis Court Oath
Rivers and Mountains
The Double Dream of Spring
Three Poems
The Vermont Notebook
Self-Portrait in a Convex Mirror
Houseboat Days
As We Know
Shadow Train
A Wave
Selected Poems

FICTION

A Nest of Ninnies
(*with James Schuyler*)

PLAYS

Three Plays

April Galleons

POEMS BY
John Ashbery

Elisabeth Sifton Books
VIKING

ELISABETH SIFTON BOOKS · VIKING
Viking Penguin Inc., 40 West 23rd Street,
New York, New York 10010, U.S.A.
Penguin Books Ltd, 27 Wrights Lane, London W8 5TZ
(Publishing & Editorial), and Harmondsworth, Middlesex,
England (Distribution & Warehouse)
Penguin Books Australia Ltd, Ringwood,
Victoria, Australia
Penguin Books Canada Limited, 2801 John Street,
Markham, Ontario, Canada L3R 1B4
Penguin Books (N.Z.) Ltd, 182–190 Wairau Road,
Auckland 10, New Zealand

First published in 1987 by Viking Penguin Inc.
Published simultaneously in Canada

Page 97 constitutes a continuation of this copyright page.

LIBRARY OF CONGRESS CATALOGING IN PUBLICATION DATA
Ashbery, John.
  April galleons.
  "Elisabeth Sifton books."
  I. Title.
PS3501.S475A86   1987   811'.54   87-40059
ISBN 0-670-81958-1

Printed in the United States of America by
Haddon Craftsmen, Scranton, Pennsylvania
Design by Ellen S. Levine
Set in Granjon

Contents

April Galleons

Vetiver

Ages passed slowly, like a load of hay,
As the flowers recited their lines
And pike stirred at the bottom of the pond.
The pen was cool to the touch.
The staircase swept upward
Through fragmented garlands, keeping the melancholy
Already distilled in letters of the alphabet.

It would be time for winter now, its spun-sugar
Palaces and also lines of care
At the mouth, pink smudges on the forehead and cheeks,
The color once known as "ashes of roses."
How many snakes and lizards shed their skins
For time to be passing on like this,
Sinking deeper in the sand as it wound toward
The conclusion. It had all been working so well and now,
Well, it just kind of came apart in the hand
As a change is voiced, sharp
As a fishhook in the throat, and decorative tears flowed
Past us into a basin called infinity.

There was no charge for anything, the gates
Had been left open intentionally.
Don't follow, you can have whatever it is.
And in some room someone examines his youth,
Finds it dry and hollow, porous to the touch.
O keep me with you, unless the outdoors
Embraces both of us, unites us, unless
The birdcatchers put away their twigs,
The fishermen haul in their sleek empty nets
And others become part of the immense crowd
Around this bonfire, a situation
That has come to mean us to us, and the crying
In the leaves is saved, the last silver drops.

Riddle Me

Rainy days are best,
There is some permanence in the angle
That things make with the ground;
In not taking off after apologies.
    The speedometer's at sundown.

Even as they spoke the sun was beginning to disappear behind a cloud.
All right so it's better to have vague outlines
But wrapped, tightly, around one's mood
Of something like vengeful joy. And in the wood
    It's all the same too.

I think I liked you better when I seldom knew you.
But lovers are like hermits or cats: they
Don't know when to come in, to stop
Breaking off twigs for dinner.
    In the little station I waited for you

And shall, what with all the interest
I bear toward plans of yours and the future
Of stars it makes me thirsty
Just to go down on my knees looking
    In the sawdust for joy.

June and the nippers will scarcely look our way.
And be bold then it's then
This cloud imagines us and all that our story
Was ever going to be, and we catch up
    To ourselves, but they are the selves of others.

And with it all the city starts to live
As a place where one can believe in moving
To a particular name and be there, and then
It's more action falling back refreshed into death.
    We can survive the storms, wearing us

Like rainbow hats, afraid to retrace steps
To the past that was only recently ours,
Afraid of finding a party there.
O in all your life were you ever teased
    Like this, and it became your mind?

Where still some saunter on the bank in mixed
Plum shade and weary sun, resigned
To the installations on the opposite bank, we mix
Breathless greetings and tears and lately taste
    The precious supplies.

Morning Jitters

And the storm reestablished itself
As a hole in the sheet of time
And of the weariness of the world,
And all the old work that remains to be done on its surface.
Came morning and the husband was back on the shore
To ask another favor of the fish,
Leviathan now, patience wearing thin. Whose answer
Bubbled out of the waves' crenellations:

"*Too late!* Yet if you analyze
The abstract good fortune that has brought you
To this floor, you must also unpluck the bees
Immured in the hive of your mind and bring the nuisance
And the glory into sharper focus. Why,
Others too will have implored before forgetting
To remove a stick of night from the scrub-forest
That keeps us wondering about ourselves
Until luck or nepotism has run its course! Only I say,
Your uniqueness isn't that unique
And doors must close in the shaved head
Before they can spring ajar. Take this.
Its promise equals power." To be shaken thus
Vehemently back into one's trance doesn't promise
Any petitioner much, even the servile ones. But night in its singleness
Of motive rewards all equally for what cannot
Appear disinterested survival tactics from the vantage
Point of some rival planet. Things go on being the same,
As darkness and ships ruffle the sky.

A Snowball in Hell

In the beginning there are those who don't quite fit in
But are somehow okay. And then some morning
There are places that suddenly seem wonderful:
Weather and water seem wonderful,
And the peaceful night sky that arrives
In time to protect us, like a sword
Cutting the blue cloak of a prince.

But one night the door opened
And there was nothing to say, the relationships
Had gotten strangely tilted, like price tags.
That girl you loved, that former patient of mine,
Arrives soused on a Monday
After the crunch it seems.
Please play this back. All the recording
In the world won't help unless you or someone else listens
At some point in time to what the mountain
Is helplessly trying to tell us, season
After season, whose streams roar fatally
In and out of one chapter in our lives.

The book was a present.
Best to throw it away, to the bottom
Of the sea where ingenuous fish may read it
Or not. A little striving here,
Some relaxation there, and no one will know the difference.
Oh, but what you said about the season—
Is it dull, or exhausting, or has it left
And will be right back with something truly splendid
For us, for once in a lifetime?

Dreams of Adulthood

Why does he do it like that say it like that you might ask
Dream it like that over landscapes spotted with cream and vehement
Holes in the ground that have become little lakes, now that the chill and
  ardor
Of winter are passing into the real thing, where we shall be obliged
To survive? That there is a precise, preordained structure
That has been turned inside out to meet new personal needs
And attract newer bonuses isn't the reply, it's the solution,
Read, the asking, so while this helps, doesn't hinder, its persona
Is off running parallel somewhere: monitorable, but that's about it.

And we see the cries of the innocent how they were coming to help
Us in the storehouse and recruit all that bad knowledge so as to save it
For brighter purposes some day. Alas, these good gestures can't help;
What is needed is a disparate account of the thing happening just now,
To have it sink finally into print, from which there is no escape, no
Never, it all just gets gradually lost for the betterment of humankind.
Think how if there were no toys, we might grow up repeating these
  encounters
With actual people, and how, much later, seriousness would get destroyed
And incorporated into the record, like sand into concrete.
And the long taffylike ribbon that oozes so perfectly
Telling us much about ourselves and those outside us and like us
Would reach its resting place in the desert sump sooner for that:
The Lake Havasu City of our dreams where London Bridge eyes the sands
Nervously, and vice versa. No, there's no shortcut to being overcharged,
And if one wants to become a diamond eventually it isn't too early
To begin thinking about it, no, to begin thinking about it right now
Before storks are actually to be observed standing on chimneys, cruelly
  one-legged,
And the tarmac of one season is brought in, brushed off and saved
For any other season: for all consequences to be minded.

My name is Steve she said my name is Brian
My pretty baa-lambs each have names just like everything else upon earth,

Proper names, I mean. This way we are allowed to recognize species
From itinerant examples of them: "Hi, my name's Joe,"
And one is instantly plugged in to the mountains of possibility
That can only refresh us if we know about how to go about letting them:
In quiet, in dove-gray silence
Where the rescuers' tools are far, far richer than they were before.
Even ghost stories are fairly prevalent, and about to be believed.
Why not, after all, with so much variation,
Such mutability in the recounting of it? Yet soon, of course,
All are bound into a uniform edition, one can't be redeemed
By any of it anymore, only darkness and truth can do that now:
The woods where we used to wander, fumbling for carob,
The *Johannisbrot* that nourished that saint in his solitude
And then came to be the food for a whole kind of being that
Still outruns us courteously, we think, what a riot of showmanship
And actual produce reimburses us now, and how we have come to be
Improved by it. You should know never to ask questions, they'll
Slap you mildly on the wrists for it, but meanwhile in your reading
You'll have the sufficient answer for why it came to be this way.
And though one might complain about certain aspects, the long fond fugue
In which one will come to observe oneself being enveloped has answers
For much else besides as it teases us over the hill into eternity
Like the Duke of York's men and then marches us back down the same
Slope with the daisies you are meant to notice. Sure was pretty
Close back there, I got scared, didn't you? The feeling that something
Enormous, like a huge canvas, is happening without one's having the
Least suspicion, without one single scrap of information being vouchsafed?
How can you live with that, even for a few years or so, they go by so fast
In patches or clusters, so that on a certain day of reckoning, not *the* one,
Every available jug or receptacle will be seen to be full to overflowing,
Not with anything useful, just the same old stuff of imaginative
Speculation as it was before and still is, unfortunately. These wisps, I
Guess I'll save them for a while. They need me, don't you think?

A Mood of Quiet Beauty

The evening light was like honey in the trees
When you left me and walked to the end of the street
Where the sunset abruptly ended.
The wedding-cake drawbridge lowered itself
To the fragile forget-me-not flower.
You climbed aboard.

Burnt horizons suddenly paved with golden stones,
Dreams I had, including suicide,
Puff out the hot-air balloon now.
It is bursting, it is about to burst
With something invisible
Just during the days.
We hear, and sometimes learn,
Pressing so close

And fetch the blood down, and things like that.
Museums then became generous, they live in our breath.

When half the time they don't
know themselves . . .

Old cathedrals, old markets, good and firm things
And old streets, one always feels intercepted
As they walk quickly past, no nonsense, cabbages
And turnips, the way they get put into songs:

One needn't feel offended
Or shut out just because the slow purpose
Under it is evident,
Because someone is simply there.

Yet it's a relief to look up
To the moist, imprecise sky,
Thrashing about in loneliness,
Inconsolable . . .

There has to be a heart to this.
The words are there already.
Just because the river looks like it's flowing backwards
Doesn't mean that motion doesn't mean something,
That it's incorrect as a metaphor.

And the way stones sink,
So gracefully,
Doesn't rob them of the dignity
Of their cantankerous gravity.

They are what they are and what they seem.
Maybe our not getting closer to them
Puts some kind of shine on us
We didn't consent to,
As though we were someone's car:
Large, animated, calm.

Adam Snow

Let's try the ingenuous mode, if for no better
Reason than its staying power: locked into a continuum
That rises and falls with the contours of this earth,
Inhabiting a Tom Tiddler's ground of special pleading
And cash-and-carry. Long lines at the checkout counter
Are a reason to behave, sad and dramatic, silhouetted
Against the tidal wave. For what must be, must be,
The old priest said, his face a maze
Of claw-prints in the snow
Which always arrives in time to antagonize
Or humor, before bedtime, it's your choice.
And suddenly outlines unlock
The forms they were sequestering, just to make it simple
And equal.

Ah, but all fakes aren't alike.
I think we must settle for the big thing
Since quality, though a matter of survival,
Is such a personal call. Sometimes it's nowhere at all
Or a faint girl will make light of it, saying
In the sprockets in the backwoods there are no noticeable
Standards, nothing to judge one or be judged by.
It's true the refreshing absence of color
Produces an effect like that of time;
That you may be running through thistles one moment
And across a sheet of thin ice the next and not be aware
Of any difference, only that you have been granted an extension.
Make sure you clean up this mess. Other than that,
Listening to widely spaced catcalls is OK
The livelong day, and sleep isn't rationed.
Yet one can only question how the system arose,
Creating itself, I suppose,
Since nothing else has yet taken the responsibility.
If it makes you happier to feel, to see the horror
Of living one's life alone for something, what the heck,

Be my guest, it takes two to tango
After all, or something, doesn't it?
And you get right back on that conveyor belt
Of dreams to tip the scale modestly
Into your own enterprise, nest egg, portfolio
Of standard greetings and uncommon manners.
The ending can't take the blame.

It read like the cubist diary of a brook
That sidled past the house one day
On its way to a rendezvous with some river
We can never cross twice. And the gradual
Escalation lay nearby: we cannot call it back
Yet may meet it again, in other times, under different auspices.

Forgotten Song

O Mary, go and call the cattle home
For I'm sick in my heart and fain would lie down.

As if that wasn't enough, I find this bundle of pain
Left on my doorstep, with a note: "Please raise it as your own."

I don't know. When it grows up will it be like the others,
Able to join in their games, or is it the new person,

As yet indescribable, though existing here and there?
Our caution can't make any sense to it. Meanwhile it erases us

In coming to be what can't possibly be for the time being,
This time we take in and lavish so much affection on

It starts to like us, changeling though it be, and sees
Some point in the way we were made. Death

Always intervenes at that moment, waking avenues
That radiate from the heart of a city whose suburbs

Are its uneasy existence. Put another way, the continual stirring
That we come to recognize as life merely acts blindly,

In pursuit of small, selfish goals, but the repercussions
Are enormous though they concern no one. Growing chooses this way

To happen, doesn't mind if a few toes get stepped on,
Though it would hardly have wished things to turn out like this

If it had thought about it for a moment. But it can't—I mean
That's what it is, a sigh of a sleeping giantess

That causes turbulence even in the shy, still unused fields
Stacked to the horizon, not even waiting, secure

In their inertia. A force erupting so violently
We can't witness any of it. Best to leave it alone

And start it all over again, if there's a beginning.
The stalk is withered dry, my love, so will our hearts decay.

Unless we omitted something. And we did. It'll cure it.
It will have to. But I can't whisper that story yet.

Finnish Rhapsody

He managed the shower, coped with the small spattering drops,
Then rubbed himself dry with a towel, wiped the living organism.
Day extended its long promise, light swept through his refuge.
But it was time for business, back to the old routine.

Many there are, a crowd exists at present,
For whom the daily forgetting, to whom the diurnal plunge
Truncates the spadelike shadows, chops off the blades of darkness,
To be rescued, to be guided into a state of something like security.
Yet it falls off for others; for some, however, it drops from sight:
The millers, winnowers of wheat,
Dusted with snow-white flour, glazed with farinaceous powder,
Like Pierrot, like the white clown of chamber music;
The leggy mannequins, models slender and tall;
The sad children, the disappointed kids.

And for these few, to this small group
Forgetting means remembering the ranks, oblivion is recalling the rows
Of flowers each autumn and spring; of blooms in the fall and early summer.
But those traveling by car, those nosing the vehicle out into the crowded
    highway
And at the posts of evening, the tall poles of declining day,
Returning satisfied, their objective accomplished,
Note neither mystery nor alarm, see no strangeness or cause for fright.
And these run the greatest risk at work, are endangered by their
    employment
Seeing there can be no rewards later, no guerdon save in the present:
Strong and severe punishment, *peine forte et dure,*
Or comfort and relaxation, coziness and tranquillity.

Don't fix it if it works, tinker not with that which runs apace,
Otherwise the wind might get it, the breeze waft it away.
There is no time for anything like chance, no spare moment for the aleatory,
Because the closing of our day is business, the bottom line already here.

One wonders what roadblocks were set up for, we question barricades:
Is it the better to time, jot down the performance time of
Anything irregular, all that doesn't fit the preconceived mold
Of our tentative offerings and withdrawals, our hesitant giving and taking
  back?
For those who perform correctly, for the accurate, painstaking ones
Do accomplish their business, get the job done,
And are seldom seen again, and are rarely glimpsed after that.
That there are a few more black carriages, more somber chariots
For some minutes, over a brief period,
Signifies business as usual, means everything is OK,
That the careful have gone to their reward, the capable disappeared
And boobies, or nincompoops, numskulls and sapheads,
Persist, faced with eventual destruction; endure to be confronted with
  annihilation someday.

The one who runs little, he who barely trips along
Knows how short the day is, how few the hours of light.
Distractions can't wrench him, preoccupations forcibly remove him
From the heap of things, the pile of this and that:
Tepid dreams and mostly worthless; lukewarm fancies, the majority of them
  unprofitable.
Yet it is from these that the light, from the ones present here that luminosity
Sifts and breaks, subsides and falls asunder.
And it will be but half-strange, really be only semi-bizarre
When the tall poems of the world, the towering earthbound poetic utterances
Invade the street of our dialect, penetrate the avenue of our patois,
Bringing fresh power and new knowledge, transporting virgin might and
  up-to-date enlightenment
To this place of honest thirst, to this satisfyingly parched here and now,
Since all things congregate, because everything assembles
In front of him, before the one
Who need only sit and tie his shoelace, who should remain seated, knotting
  the metal-tipped cord

For it to happen right, to enable it to come correctly into being
As moments, then years; minutes, afterwards ages
Suck up the common strength, absorb the everyday power
And afterwards live on, satisfied; persist, later to be a source of gratification,
But perhaps only to oneself, haply to one's sole identity.

Forgotten Sex

They tore down the old movie palaces,
Ripped up streetcar tracks, widened avenues.
Lampposts, curbs with their trees vanished.

They knew, who came after,
A story of departing hands and affairs, that mostly
Went untold, unless someone who was there once
Visited the old neighborhood, and then
They would tell about it, the space
Of an afternoon, how it happened in the afternoon
So that no record, no print of it could exist
For the steep times to come. And sure enough,
Even as the story ended its shadow vanished,
A twice-told tale not to be told again
Unless children one day dig up the past, in the attic
Or under brush in the back yard: "What's this?"
And you have to tell them, will have to tell them then
That the enormous nature of things had a face
Once and feet like any human being, and one day
Broke out of the shell that had always been,
Changed its answers to lies, youthful ambition
To a quirk of the past, a fancy, of some
Antiquarian concern that this damaged day can never
Countenance if we want to live past the rope
Of noon, reach the bald summits by late afternoon.

Surely we are protected, surely someone thinks of us
Often enough to keep the stain from setting, surely
All of us are alike and know each other from earliest
Childhood, for better or for worse: surely we eat
Breakfast each day, and shit, and put the kettle on the stove
With much changing of the subject, much twisting the original
Premise back to the nature of the actual itch
Engulfing us, now. And when we come back
From an outing expect to find the furniture magically

Rearranged to accommodate revised, smaller projects
No one bothers to question, except polite Puss-in-Boots with what
Is in effect a new premise: "Try this one, the dust
Shows less on these rather sad colors; the time
To get started and gain time, however brief, over the neighbors
Quarreling into sunset, once you have convinced them you're
Not playing and therefore not cheating. When the princess
Comes to see you on some perfectly plausible pretext, you'll know
The underground stream that has never stood still is the surface
And the theater for all that is to come. Too bad the revisions
Will never be adopted, but how lucky for you, now,
The change of face. Good times follow bad."

And the locket is still on the chain on a throat.
The askers, the doers, fall into silent confusion
As it comes time to stand up like a sheet of metal
In the blast of sunrise. I will do this, I can do no more.
I cannot think on the edge of a platform.

But the abandonment by love is a de facto sign
Of something else coming along,
Something similar in its measuredness:
Sweetness of things late, a memory for particulars
As lively as though they happened still. As indeed
They do sometimes, though like the transparent bricks
In a particular dream, they cannot always be seen.

Insane Decisions

Somehow I always do manage but
You *found* them for me, what
I love, lakes and paintings.

In the night it slipped its mooring.
By daybreak they were gone.
All I did was let the kettle boil.
The familiar silhouette
Kept me from thinking about it.

It's vestigial.
Nothing is missing.
So everything is OK,
Houses markedly more modest,
On and on and on.
A view of the parking lot.

Certain frequencies
Haven't abandoned it yet.
You can still find those pleasures somewhere,
In old stalls. Negative
Listener response hasn't drowned
The very simple thing of this world
We were taught to respect
As we were growing up.
Comma in the eye of God.
The desired effect.

No I Don't

I have no adventures, the adventurous one began,
Except for my hearing, which as you know, can be undependable.
Sometimes staying in the house can be bad. But then, returning,
To find some vine that has licked out over an eave
Like an unruly eyebrow, something that wasn't there
Moments ago, can stop you in your tracks. I mean the way
Things have of just happening once the principle
Of happening has been laid down for them can be alarming
Or like a rush of bubbles to the nose, depending. Mostly
Faces are good to me though, I lap them up like lukewarm tea.

Only when the giant's last belch has been duly heard
And recorded can we proceed with the meeting; by then, however,
Its processes are swamped in the atmosphere of the tale
It seems we overheard, taking on a new, irregular life
From it, hauling our drab sensibilities away with it
Until it reads like autobiography. Wasn't it on this day
Exactly a year ago, that the fabric began to rustle
And strange stems with small gilded flowers on them were suddenly
There, and obviously the seeds had been planted at some point
For it to happen, so much of it as it's only now
Turning out to seem? Our fathers, who had so many categories
For so few things, could have supplied a term
Like a special brush for bathing, and in due course this
Particularity would have faded into the sum of the light,
An entity no more. But we perceive it as another kind of thing,
From another order, neither familiar nor strange but rooted
In the near future, muzzle lowered like a charging beast's,
But a hint, shadow of an approaching season, so there's
Some fun in that. Mostly bother and having to get up,
It's true, but not without moments of amusement that stay
Like a thin, spreading stain on white muslin: the commodity
Of our dreams, it turns out, but also something we could sell
If we wanted to, before it slips out to sea like a great, rusted ship.

But you—
You cannot follow them, he said,
You have to stay here just one more day please
To take the reading so that all who might have been relieved
By your definite verdict may catch pleasurable breaths again
And say it's so. It registered. True, this leaves us with little to do:
Housework, or something called that. Changing the needle
Of the clock, putting the dust away in twos and threes
As icons merge with the old gold of twilight: you,
A person to be read to. Then the bargains
In knotted ribbons in the sky, as sincerely blue-violet as the deep
Thoughts of their maker, can stun without hurting, emptying
Us out of sleep's dustpan into the little pile of question
Marks and wooden letters, and night gets sleepy
And silly, what with all those peculiar noises. Doesn't it come on
Faster though? And aren't the apes more impatient for a sign
From the passion flower, whether it will or will not hang
The "closed" sign at the door for whatever may be good in us
That will last as long as death: a polite closed one?

Posture of Unease

It all seems like dirt now.
There is a film of dust on the lucid morning
Of an autumn landscape, that must be worse
Where it's tightening up,
Where not everything has its own two feet to stand on.

It gets more and more simplistic:
Good and bad, evil and bad; what else do we know?
Flavors that keep us from caring too long.

But there was that train of thought
That satisfied one nicely: how one was going to climb down
Out of here, hopefully
To arrive on a perfectly flat spit of sand
Level with the water.

And everything would look new and worn again.
Suddenly, a shout, a convincing one.
People in twos and threes turn up, and
There's more to it than that.

But for all you I
Have neglected, ignored,
Left to stew in your own juices,
Not been that friend that is approaching,
I ask forgiveness, a song new like rain.
Please sing it to me.

Alone in the Lumber Business

It's still too early to make concessions.
Meanwhile the long night glided on,
Intent on some adventure of its own, like a dog
Dreaming of a bone. But under the coat of burrs

Lay the stones, and they were awake, desire
Still shriveled in the bud, but they were there,
Soon to be on fire. As the tree beautifies itself
Over a period of several months, all things

Take up their abode in the questions it asks,
And don't even dream of them, perhaps. Poor, misguided pilgrim,
It says, overtaken by every new tempest
That comes along, your cloak, the half you kept, caked with mud.

Life, it thinks, is like growing up
Entrusted to the sole care of a French governess,
Never knowing anything about your parents,
As lights come on in the city far across the bay.

Then it's suddenly an orgy of name-giving,
Of hyphenated names, names with "Dr." attached to them,
The flowers waiting to be named, the days
Of the month, and so on. And the medicines.

And it's like not being grown up anymore,
Like being a fifty-seven-year-old child or something,
The secret having leaked out again. No
Name quite sticks. Wine and cider

Taste like Chinese-restaurant tea.
One has cobbled a kind of life together,
The cloud and outlines of the sod
Still glowing, longing to touch you with the fire

That shapes us, then replaces us on the shelf.
It's safe around here though. Something
In the darkness understands, tries to make up for it all.
But it's like a new disease, a resistant strain.

Where were you when it was all happening?
Night is full of kindred spirits now,
Voices, photos of loved ones, faces
Out of the newspaper, eager smiles blown like leaves

Before they become fungus. No time to give credit
Where it is due, though actions, as before,
Speak louder than words. To dot the i's,
Cross the t's and tie everything up

In a loose bundle stamped "not wanted on the voyage."
There were flowers in a garden once,
Monkey business, shenanigans. But it all
Gets towered over. There would be no point

In replying to the finer queries, since we live
In our large, square, open landscape. The bridge
Of fools once crossed, there are adjustments to be made.
But you have to settle in to looking at these things.

Vaucanson

It was snowing as he wrote.
In the gray room he felt relaxed and singular,
But no one, of course, ever trusts these moods.

There had to be understanding to it.
Why, though? That always happens anyway,
And who gets the credit for it? Not what is understood,
Presumably, and it diminishes us
In our getting to know it

As trees come to know a storm
Until it passes and light falls anew
Unevenly, on all the muttering kinship:
Things with things, persons with objects,
Ideas with people or ideas.

It hurts, this wanting to give a dimension
To life, when life is precisely that dimension.
We are creatures, therefore we walk and talk
And people come up to us, or listen
And then move away.

Music fills the spaces
Where figures are pulled to the edges,
And it can only say something.

Sinews are loosened then,
The mind begins to think good thoughts.
Ah, this sun must be good:
It's warming again,
Doing a number, completing its trilogy.
Life must be back there. You hid it
So no one would find it
And now you can't remember where.

But if one were to invent being a child again
It might just come close enough to being a living relic
To save this thing, save it from embarrassment
By ringing down the curtain,

And for a few seconds no one would notice.
The ending would seem perfect.
No feelings to dismay,
No tragic sleep to wake from in a fit
Of passionate guilt, only the warm sunlight
That slides easily down shoulders
To the soft, melting heart.

Unreleased Movie

Let's start in the middle, as usual. Ever since I burnt my mouth
I talk two ways, first as reluctant explainer, then as someone offstage
In a dream, hushing those who might wake you from this dream,
Imperfectly got up as a lutanist. Then sighs, whirrs, screeches
Become so much its fabric that one listens to see what words materialize
On the windowpane this time. I don't want to make an uneasy habit
Of this though, because when the universe does turn into a horror movie
It will mean Japanese undershirts for the kiddies and unusual, invisible
Demerits for those of us caught talking back at the screen, unless, of course,
The unnatural peace God predicted for us has settled like a giant shell
Over the ocean floor, in which case we shall all be forgiven and forgotten,
Like students in a correspondence school. And I mean what shall be saved
Of us as we live aimed at some near but unattainable mark on the wall?
Not, one fears, a thing of hitherto unheard-of compacted density
That might relieve all the years with spaces in them, years of leggy growth,
Too much foliage, the wrong light, the wrong taste to things.

There is so much we know, too much, cruelly, to be expressed in any
  medium,
Including silence. And to harbor it means having it eventually leach under
The spiritual retaining wall that so commends itself to us we can never
Be other, and become a different habitat altogether in which these transactions
Are the brittle sounds of insect wings, robbed of the solid clink of something
Like the reality that now accosts one. It is all, we see too late, a question
Of having the knack, but the knack is as universal as the wind that now
  protects,
Now buffets, and is not ours. Thus, we are more formal this year, can escape
Certain confrontations, obtain the release of certain compromised acquaintances
Without looking at what they may have become, foil the plans of a few
Middle-echelon apparatchiks until the day that finally does come to rest, busily,
At your doorstep. Put it into a clean jar. Save it from the time which
Has been, without promoting it too far beyond the venetian blind of that
Future's early demise, in which we saw ourselves prefigured dimly and what
  would
Happen to us scattered all over the ground like bruised rinds. Only say what

Cannot be done to us, for now, and keep us ever straying over the border into
Insanity and back, and by then, becalmed, we shall know the superior disci-
    pline
As something lived within us, something that magnetizes everything toward us.
But beware the merely frivolous gesture, token of its own smile, which
    clamps
One supremely to one's own past, in which one is lost. Better the negative
Volumes of the lives of strangers carried out to a certain point just this side of
Emptiness, so as to be done with it. And those who may be hungry, or thirsty,
Or tired; those who lived in a landscape without fully understanding it, may,
By their ignorance and needing help blossom again in the same season into
    a new
Angle or knot, without feeling unwanted again. So, at any rate, it is written
And believed by some few, a hundred or maybe a thousand of the summarily
    instructed.

Doors will forever bang in that wind, night moths assault the screens until
We know what we are thinking about once more. And that day may guide us.
So the dream curved back into something natural (it always does!), beached us
Where we started, furious at being safe and sound again. The old oarlocks
Encased in moss, the same tire marks in the gravel. And we come together
To quarrel or make love without any memory of the crabbed ambitions that
    were there
Before us, and may outlive us but we shan't know this, it won't make any
    difference
Even tonight as I lie here placing a finger now on one page of the book, now
On another, as though by planting it there I might outgrow the busy destiny
Predicted in those teeming lines. Really, it makes no difference:
If we are all going to be one, or together, in the space between the moment
I had this imperfect vision and tomorrow. Yet, as marble
Dust is gradually brushed away one does come upon it, that split-second
Interval as formal as a jewel, that an army of well-meaning enemies couldn't
Possibly displace. I hear it calling to me. I must turn over a new leaf.
It is the extreme last chance for doing so. I want it so much. And then the
    world is

Shredded as a blanket waiting for this to happen, returns to it like a kiss,
To that agreeable triangle in a sea of asphalt where one so rarely has difficulty
Getting a taxi, and all magic works, the wicked and the only misguided.
I am re-created in the short-sleeved pajamas of my youth.

Disguised Zenith

"All to do, all over again,
  And if I had it..." Light fills a corner
Of the room, not paying attention
To the racing wind outside,
                              the aching white powder.
Yes, there are Pierrots and Pierrots,
She resumed, but the wind makes maggots of us all,
Flies on a wall, and there is no meaning but in suffering
And where is the suffering in that?

All the beautiful crafts, the tint choicer
Than the rest, are available "at all times," but
We decode them backwards,
Their meaning is *for* our meaning, and where
Is the meaning in that?
Like a long teatime, a stroll
Downward over lawns, always more plumed
And malicious. Did I have you
There, that one time,
And do I have you lost now,
More steady, like a jar
Marveling at its own emptiness, yet you shall taste it,
A sea breeze one day glimpsed,
Taken away, but you never knew you had it
And so notice nothing strange, its absence
Is perfect, and the room suddenly is lighter.
It is really light in this fold. You know why.

Railroad Bridge

My relatives asked me over. Because I know
How everything is always becoming a lot of things,
Then a few one can keep track of
And they become more bored and trivial
Until the main issue lies sincere again,
Sweet as spring.

The problem then is its high readability.
She knew how to go. He was interested
In some arts project. Listening to a Sunday
Afternoon philharmonic concert amid tulips
And freesias, you get right out of it,
Right off the page. The reader is reading your brain,
That fluid but even surface. No scar
Resolves it. From pentimenti to waste water
All the subjects have been scanned.
The sewers are clogged. A wide way
Of evading contracts to a point and darkens,
And the audience, kids mostly, can carry this
To the distant trees. Can digest the meat.

But, as so often happens in the world of literature,
The tables are turned.
Why is life a tidal basin and tutors
That can correct you only after you've corrected them?
Only in dreams as an airplane sometimes rises
Do you get the feeling that some of this is good for you,
That if you stay put something good will happen
To your next-door neighbor's daughter and what will
That role have been? Tourist? Consumer? Strong
Confidante? It's still screened, simply thrilling
Though sheep leak out like creeks lost
In a riverbed and someone is coming to see about that.
And how many actresses will that make?

Who wants to play you? Your life snowballed
And hardened and after that there was nothing
To do except wait for colors to leach through
Layers of old paint and scold the witness,
Calling down unimaginable tantrums on his head.

The dopey shuttle still fidgets among taut
Wires. Life in New York was pleasant in those days.

October at the Window

Do I really want to go to the city?
Here there are light and cats
And birds that live in the sky
And metal that must be painted or
It will rust, that causes deep brooding
Down among the plants and whatever insects
And small animals there are there.

A splash of snow bursts along
Green buildings and the emptiness opens
Out along my arms like a magic thing,
A specimen of some kind. Always
There are instances, like the sea,
The sky, and paper. The landscape is too long
For what it will accommodate (towers,
The lack of cold). The posthumous spyglass
Of the author lies, alert. The works
Of Thomas Lovell Beddoes fall open
And are sick and alive, books of iron, and faintly gilded
In the dim light of the early nineteenth century.
Someone traveled there once, and observed
Accurately, and became "the observer,"
But with so much else to do
This figure too got lost, charged
In the night, to say what had to be said:

"My eyes are bigger than my stomach."
And so life goes on happening
As in a frontier novel. One must always
Be quite conscious of the edges of things
And then how they meet will cease
To be an issue, all other things
Being equal, as in fact they are.
But do these complex attitudes
Compete successfully with the sounds

Of bedlam and the overhead lighting there
Of which Clare wrote so accurately
"But still I read and sighed and sued again,"
Noting in despair the times of day,
The hair of fields, the way we go
Willingly into another's arms and back?

Wrack bleaches on tidal sand.
A moth is caught in my lamp
To make it light the true way,
Pastel fields where only
He who comes to save says the single,
Enameled word that outlives us.
That there are flowers in shacks, broken
Mirrors among fallen doorposts
Doesn't trip us up so much, rather
It's the lesson, unlearned, whose wry whimper,
Hidden among congruent pages, tells
The story of how we were and how we were meant to be.

No Two Alike

Wait—it has some kind of finish on it. No
Point in overreacting, since the effect
Is, in effect, not overdone. There are scars and stars,
Things to be met with in life, a lifetime of slow defeat
Spent sitting outdoors, propped against a wall,
Eating day-old bread. And then the world changed.

No one expected it would be like this.
Yet we are calmer, and safer, for it,
As though some big man had come in, and turned
And abruptly left in the few moments I was out.
Those are people in the street, the ones you passed.
Who can say if it's empty or clear? That
Patina got on it, and was what mattered for a while.

In groves in England you think there must be some
Superior kind of stretching, some way to go
That is not moving off at all. Some ministering
To the handy and the articulate, and bread left then
Won't be idle, part of a mass of frayed circumstance.
Water would rise coolly toward the throat then.

Pray that in just one bubble the color
Will cover the whole surface sheen,
Polluting remembrance, the house where I was born.
And in that moment of curious rage an attic
Is pitched, a place to come after long love,
And dexterity after wearing these fingers out.

Amid Mounting Evidence

I was reading about dinosaurs:
Once the scratching phase is over, and the mirage
Or menage has begun, and the world lies open
To the radiation theory (tons of radiation, think of it,
Reversing all normal procedures
So that the pessimistic ball of wax begins
To slide down the inclined plane again
Bringing further concepts to their doom while encouraging
The infinity of loose ends that
Is taking over our government and threatening to become life as we know it!)
It is time to slink off to one's post in some cold desert
(Not the Sahara, more like the Gobi actually)
And wait amid that sadness known as banishment
For the point to reappear, though it may never do so,
And what was that strange uniform?

Only that we lived happily in ever-after land
And the fire of my mind was still with us then
Prevented the object of these negotiations from becoming a toy
Farther down the keyboard (and of course this did happen
Later on, every potential is realized if one waits long enough,
Only by that time the context may have faded, fragile
As summersweet or the light on a windowsill, and then,
And then, why the text will be seen as regular
Only no one wants to play anymore; games
Have their fashions much as truth does) and our lives from
Being turned into a shambles too large to deal with, unreasonable;
And as masonry weathers, as moths are silently at work in blankets
Even as you read this, I saw no reason for complaint
Or murmur and the entourage liked me, agreeing
With me that this wasn't the right time or place,
That arguments would be foreshortened if initiated now.
Yet this toothache that never seems to go away,
Burning mildly through the night, heartbeat

Of something, augurs no calamity unless leagues
And leagues of silent forest canopied by matte-gray
Sky are to be construed as such, but I think our peace
Should be given the benefit of a doubt and allowances
Surely made for all our thoughts and daily activities
If peace is what we really want, Roman
Candles ripping open the evening notwithstanding.
It's so easy to trudge and pretend to be a boy
When deep down what you want is asking,
Not rich assurances that are autumnal
In the way they finally work out and become a sad
Though voluminous and vital commentary on our standing
Impatiently, waiting for the weather to make the first move,
And when this happens, be the first to scurry away
Complaining inaudibly and in general installing
Oneself as a capital nuisance, never to be given the time of day again.

And if this should happen there are always windows
With flower boxes and dreamy young girls just behind them.
There are birds who stop by for one last agitated farewell
Before the long flight to the south, and so much more
To prevent the ultimatum from being drawn up that really
In the first falling flakes a job does get done:
Energy left over from some previous and saucy commitment
Turns out not to have been such a bad option. The drilling
Of noon insects in high summer had to precede this or something
Else, the dream be given texture and further substance
Because of something. It seems
Shipshape now. Everything seems to be all right.
The storm, you see, told none of its secrets,
Gave nothing away. There would have been no one to repeat it to
In any case. And the signs of stress that follow
In the wake of confusion are there to be read, but the electricity
Bakes them into shapes of its own cognizance, its wanting

To give us something a little better to spend
The rest of our lives looking for, wondering whether it got misplaced.
In the old days this would have been on the house.

Letters I Did or Did Not Get

Because whenever we go somewhere we
Don't know how long it will be till we get back
This specter of progress was invented:
Time on my hands, nothing to do (more
Unexpected than startling, in fact). A sleepy giant
In his cave can feel the bowels twitch,
The shudder. Darkness inspires him
To deeds that could later turn out to be misdeeds,
Yet that prompting is valuable, scorches in each one
Of us the impulse to be overridden later.
Then we too smile, in sunlight. It's going
To be later than ever, this time, we know that,
But the facts around us are so charming.
One feels time and space as a gift
In these insect moments, hidden from sight,
An arena where actors playing drunken slaves
Can fart and bellow at the audience, and everything
At the end will be whitewashed, that is incidents
Will glimmer through layers and layers of paint,
Enough to keep one occupied at least,
Until the end of the performance
When each is transported to an individual dream
And the business of living can begin again.

Oh, sometimes it would seem as though storms
Might wash some of it away, some
Nastiness or other one was hoping to keep
From others as well as from oneself.
And these came and went, and other teasing
Events fitted in between. Invitations were sent out
Yet none was ever known to arrive
And in the end it seemed the same old cellar hole
Was where one was vainly taking refuge
Again and not telling others about it lest
It become too popular and be flooded

With emotions before the original shack was torn down.
The father-and-son banquet scheduled for this holiday
Eve was going to take place and dour but glowing
Testimonials to the truth of some knowledgeable
Person or situation be read aloud: please,
No publicity or flowers
Or we might have to cancel the rest of each of our lives
In order for curfew to ring again; otherwise
Be glad the flowers at least pretend to take an interest
In our shapes. Yet too soon the leaves are whipped away,
There was no point in standing up for them
Either, but winter
Will kiss our eyes awake
And surely the long struggle to get here
Will lie picturesquely unfolded on the grass
For all to see. Our varied accomplishments
Take over when time ceases; our
Credits dusted off, buffed to a dull gold smear,
Will glow against the brown holland of eternity.
Surely, then, someone will come to ask
Of us, knocking at the door, pulling the latch chain
To open into fire and breathing our very own
Unedited tale of how it happened,
Of each step that led away from childhood
To the bounteous past before us now,
Wild towers springing up in the white gloom—

Bedtime is calling,
The sea overwhelms the shore,
Sandmen approach on weary steps,
Wanting to be with us, again, for the millionth time,
Yet nothing is known of all this,
How the sad voyage began in the morning
And the wheels locked in late afternoon
Before a child came to release us.

There are too many of us ever
To be remembered let alone recorded
But when we think the gramophone has finished playing
It whistles, calling from far away
To participate in whatever is fanciful
About the ending: drinking "weak tea
With only a very little milk, and no sugar":
Mystery and death, the way you like it.

Frost

Trapped in the wrong dream, you turn
Out of an alley into a wide, weak street   Mirrors
Fall from trees, and it could be time
To refinance the mess of starting
And staying put. But rumors feed this.
The distant passage is then always sublime
And well-lit for some, a curious picture
Of longing and distress for others.

Meanwhile the only tall thing
Of importance dismantles himself,
Transparent in places, sometimes opaque
And more beautiful for the scenes
That might be projected on him. The secret
Chamber is one, where only the king
Could come, and now two or three young people
Can sit, uneasy and comfortable, discussing
Bicycles, the bone: any of the smaller anythings.
Which is quite nice, but darkness
Seems to fall more quickly, to accrue more in this sudden
Place, made of a name cut out of a map.

One gets closer to nervousness then.
It needn't be so. Things are stranger elsewhere.
Here in the dark the keeping of secrets
Is dense, that's all. There are still a few common
Names for things around; even they don't have to be
Used. Only I wish
There was some way of not getting more thoughtful,
Of not bruising the obvious shadow for which
There is a reason. Am I poor?
Have I worn out God's welcome?
There is enough dark green to cover us,
Yet will we always be speechless to the end,
Unable to say the familiar things?

Life as a Book That Has Been Put Down

We have erased each letter
And the statement still remains vaguely,
Like an inscription over the door of a bank
With hard-to-figure-out Roman numerals
That say perhaps too much, in their way.

Weren't we being surrealists? And why
Did strangers at the bar analyze your hair
And fingernails, as though the body
Wouldn't seek and find that most comfortable position,
And your head, that strange thing,
Become more problematic each time the door was shut?

We have talked to each other,
Taken each thing only just so far,
But in the right order, so it is music,
Or something close to music, telling from afar.
We have only some knowledge,
And more than the required ambition
To shape it into a fruit made of cloud
That will protect us until it goes away.

But the juice thereof is bitter,
We have not such in our gardens,
And you should go up into knowledge
With this careless sarcasm and be told there
For once, it is not here.
Only the smoke stays,
And silence, and old age
That we have come to construe as a landscape
Somehow, and the peace that breaks all records,
And singing in the land, delight
That will be and does not know us.

Too Happy, Happy Tree

If the green felicity sits too readily on the lower lip,
Other transports are by moments coolly meditative,
Choosing to tour the back lot again.
Though truly its glottal stop is the prize,
The only one, and has been down to these poor accretions
Of light and shadow, patched and sometimes perfect.

What say we get down to business, tree
That you are, knowing nothing like you
As somber and reserved as the time for flight approaches.

Was that you on the banks of the Tigris
And again halfheartedly dipping suckers in the Monongahela?
Generations of reciters told the tale
From the factory of your worn roots
And it made some difference because look how multiplied
Everything is. Your own image refracts
Again and again greeting you at embarrassed moments in the silent
History: how we were all going to be lovers
When a climatic change occurred. Years later
We again met at that solemn place of confluence,
Now worn, a seeming nub,
To parlay some advantage and get home safe with one's
Gobbet of dream for that night.
Waking up in the washtub of a West Coast moraine
You climb off your mate, check for fractures
And lo how nobly businesslike and ordinary everything
Seems to him again. This is the place we set out for
From this place and nothing the whistles or the conductor urge
Can make it over into a compact now.

Which is a good thing because winds are again restless,
Posting one to this night's relay, rendezvous
With the ghost of a shipwreck
Whose long hair is drowning—

Defeat us, we who struggled in cold for a glimpse
Of you passing by and were not disappointed
Though you seemed tired as well as noble.
In the end your narrative lost us
(How much branching out can one take?)
Until we ourselves got sloughed off in lethal considerations
Relating to size and hurricanes and the fulcrum
Of inevitable voyages to be accomplished or not.
How does it add up? You are going to parry this
With a very simple proposition and by then it will be time for
More edicts, no shoes.
And one lopes along the path
Thinking, forcibly, and by evening we have become the eye,
Blind, because it does the seeing.
It kind of makes it stand out from the rest.

Song of the Windshield Wipers

We've kept these old things
To practice on. Susie is coming in to the city,
Strange city, to have dinner with us.
Or of how a chimney, any chimney, will
Need attention some day (all those bricks
Way up in the air) or a peach
Will finally be ignored when ripe (so
Many disappointments, we can't
Keep track of them, no bother). Thus when appearances
Do decide to vote for reality
The atmosphere will have changed. It doesn't enthuse
Any more. And towers, things
Standing straight up out of it
Won't say, having been willed to be obelisks
By some force which confuses them
With diviners of structural entities
That are potentially embarrassing.

So nothing comes to surprise us
In our old city. Walking along, a noise was heard.
I thought I recognized one new building
That wasn't there a week, two weeks, maybe a month before:
All blue awnings and the proud name of some
Minor French city on it. But this
Dream too was taken away, forcibly, as though by hand.
Now one of us is lucky if he or she
Gets enough cheese, cheese-as-architecture,
I'm imagining. And few probably do,
Like the last time I was elected,
They ran to us. We were stranded on a beach,
Uninspiring. The almost-full moon
Yawned, we could see it had other places
To be, yet was loath to depart
And we began then to climb
Just to see what it is.

In the old way its look
Still pretty much dominates: what were we to be paid
Anyway, without a currency of comfort and bad habits
To be the standard of it, port from
Which false hopes could put out
And strange news from all over the world
Follow us to our lair
Where we do the loving, and are sure.
Meanwhile tentacles of the black rain
That is always outside, always, cannot
Devour us again. Better to be lodged near
In some kind of sense of here (did you
Say ear?) than be allowed to blow against a wall,
Dangerous, yet above all innocent
The way that is understood
In miles and miles
Of calendulas staked out, issuing from
Here, our backbones, and not want
To leave us, but we chide
It and growing comes
To us like play, clay
Baked that day, that is to say, to be dry,
Lonely or happy as the times will have it.
I've talked so much to you.
You don't know these people well.

The Mouse

I like what you have given me,
O my songs, scalloped chessmen
Of emotions or of elaborate indifference.
Your determining factor is a thing like the weather
That comes and goes, and stays,
What we lean out of, and into
While it arrives, deaf and gracious.
And the houses that are no more savor vividly
The lace that straps it to time, that
Slowly burning cylinder.

You see it ignites even deliberate
Apathetic lies.
What is solemn in each of us
Is forced to stand and defend
Other interests like the staging of it.
One whirls like a leaf
Without and within rain, there is no imagining
The cruelty, yet forbearance looks steep
To us now, all that planning.
Who did they think would be taken in by it?

Because the definiteness is cruel,
Makes everything shipshape. Do
I think of taking your hand,
Spiced recollections zeroing in?
But someone recommended a dim polaroid.
The square is empty now, and furred with snow,
That we used to get off at, our favorite
Stop though we didn't know it then
When all parents could lean together,
Open to what is ominous
And still stays banded within the old frame.

Song: "Mostly Places . . ."

The quarries are closed now,
The terse, blue stone is no longer mined there.
What in sleep was called imagination
No longer grazes there.

Outdoors the light is almost always better.
What fern is it you wanted to name?
Or shouldn't there be a no-name,
Or room for two, just enough for two?

And why does the humble packet of seeds
The gardener plants erupt into cold pockets of fire
On the horizon at night?
You see there is a more abrupt truth

That preempts whatever this moment is taking,
The hors d'oeuvres this moment is preparing.
Thus we lusted after it idly
Only because it was happening along,

Its charm all gone, the appeals
Speechless and opaque. Now there is no one,
No lover for you, only the wide dented metal
Of the harbor. Everyone is asleep but one.

Mostly places reject us,
Though sounds, something like a bell,
Can cut you out. Or later
In the collage of industrial noise,

In these tenements, life is twinned
As fuzzy tabloids promised.
And hark, someone is spinning her song
Out of wool and lamb's grease,

Just as the maidens had said.
With nothing but rockets to keep you awake
Small wonder the storm collapses
With a roar like chains snapping, like

The glissandi of eternity,
Tubas, triangles fetched alight in the
Not bright glare for you to be
Sure to see, you can't miss seeing

It fall this time. And the boats mere
Colored wedges like bats. That's
What you get for crying
When you're safe and sound for miles

And nobody asked you to justify whatever.
We stay far from the beaches now,
Pretend nobody cares about us,
That colors are that simple, and lines brittle.

Sighs and Inhibitions

Starting well after the beginning, one invests
The compromise quite early with nullifying
Codicils and postscripts that take the form
Of ridiculous complaints about hats and gravy
And then the way trees are organized
In the streets, complaints about the traffic,
To more general reflections:

On the way life manages itself, though its beginning
And end seem clear enough as givens, as does
The quasi-permanent siesta of noon that our long day
Is fabricated of, which stretches
In all directions to the simplifying horizon. Still,
You argue, there has to be something more solid
Than all this:

Some angle or hinge
Bulkier than stone and more resilient than the ideas
That have helped to put it across, palmed it off
On us as it were, so it is it, not we,
That is our lives, the surface over which we move
Comfortably as across a globe that gives back
Our intuiting of it as we desired it:
Lost, out in the cold,
But summonable, sometimes, when you want it.
It still knows one's name, keeps track of birthdays,
Yet is somehow foreign the way one's first language
Would be if one had grown up bilingual, and it is this other
Block-letter language we must carry (and it
Grows heavier), and place around to form the words
No one is going to understand, let alone believe,
And these account for our day, today.

I remember in the schoolyard throwing a small rock
At some kid I hated, and then, when the blood began

To ooze definitively, trying to hug the teacher,
The boy, the world, into ignoring what I'd done,
To lie and thus escape through a simple
Canceling, not a confession, to wipe the slate clean
So as to inhabit another world in which
I bore no responsibility for my acts: life
As a clear, living dream.

And I have not been spared this
Dreadful state of affairs, no one has, so that
When we think we think, or turn over in our sleep,
Someone else's business is boldly attached to this,
And there is no time for a reckoning.
The carpet never stretches quite far enough,
There is always a footfall on the stair.

Someone You Have Seen Before

It was a night for listening to Corelli, Geminiani
Or Manfredini. The tables had been set with beautiful white cloths
And bouquets of flowers. Outside the big glass windows
The rain drilled mercilessly into the rock garden, which made light
Of the whole thing. Both business and entertainment waited
With parted lips, because so much new way of being
With one's emotion and keeping track of it at the same time
Had been silently expressed. Even the waiters were happy.

It was an example of how much one can grow lustily
Without fracturing the shell of coziness that surrounds us,
And all things as well. "We spend so much time
Trying to convince ourselves we're happy that we don't recognize
The real thing when it comes along," the Disney official said.
He's got a point, you must admit. If we followed nature
More closely we'd realize that, I mean really getting your face pressed
Into the muck and indecision of it. Then it's as if
We grew out of our happiness, not the other way round, as is
Commonly supposed. We're the characters in its novel,
And anybody who doubts that need only look out of the window
Past his or her own reflection, to the bright, patterned,
Timeless unofficial truth hanging around out there,
Waiting for the signal to be galvanized into a crowd scene,
Joyful or threatening, it doesn't matter, so long as we know
It's inside, here with us.

But people do change in life,
As well as in fiction. And what happens then? Is it because we think nobody's
Listening that one day it comes, the urge to delete yourself,
"Take yourself out," as they say? As though this could matter
Even to the concerned ones who crowd around,
Expressions of lightness and peace on their faces,
In which you play no part perhaps, but even so
Their happiness is for you, it's your birthday, and even
When the balloons and fudge get tangled with extraneous

Good wishes from everywhere, it is, I believe, made to order
For your questioning stance and that impression
Left on the inside of your pleasure by some bivalve
With which you have been identified. Sure,
Nothing is ever perfect enough, but that's part of how it fits
The mixed bag
Of leftover character traits that used to be part of you
Before the change was performed
And of all those acquaintances bursting with vigor and
Humor, as though they wanted to call you down
Into closeness, not for being close, or snug, or whatever,
But because they believe you were made to fit this unique
And valuable situation whose lid is rising, totally
Into the morning-glory-colored future. Remember, don't throw away
The quadrant of unused situations just because they're here:
They may not always be, and you haven't finished looking
Through them all yet. So much that happens happens in small ways
That someone was going to get around to tabulate, and then never did,
Yet it all bespeaks freshness, clarity and an even motor drive
To coax us out of sleep and start us wondering what the new round
Of impressions and salutations is going to leave in its wake
This time. And the form, the precepts, are yours to dispose of as you will,
As the ocean makes grasses, and in doing so refurbishes a lighthouse
On a distant hill, or else lets the whole picture slip into foam.

Ostensibly

One might like to rest or read,
Take walks, celebrate the kitchen table,
Pat the dog absentmindedly, meanwhile
Thinking gloomy thoughts—so many separate
Ways of doing, one is uncertain
How the future is going to handle this.
Will it reveal itself again,
Or only in the artificial calm
Of one person's resolve to do better
Yet strike a harder bargain,
Next time?

Gardeners cannot make the world
Nor witches undo it, yet
The mad doctor is secure
In his thick-walled laboratory,
Behind evergreen borders black now
Against the snow, precise as stocking seams
Pulled straight again. There is never
Any news from that side.

A rigidity that may well be permanent
Seems to have taken over. The pendulum
Is stilled; the rush
Of season into season ostensibly incomplete.
A perverse order has been laid
There at the joint where the year branches
Into artifice one way, into a votive
Lassitude the other way, but that is stalled:
An old discolored snapshot
That soon fades away.

And so there is no spectator
And no agent to cry Enough,
That the battle chime is stilled,

The defeated memory gracious as flowers
And therefore also permanent in its way—
I mean they endure, are always around,
And even when they are not, their names are,
A fortified dose of the solid,
Livable adventure.

And from growing dim, the coals
Fall alight. There are two ways to be.
You must try getting up from the table
And sitting down relaxed in another country
Wearing red suspenders
Toward one's own space and time.

Becalmed on Strange Waters

In the presence of both, each mistook
The other's sincerity for an elaborate plot.
And perhaps something like that did occur—who knows?
There was some hostility, hostility
In the way they talked together
As the drops of warm liquor went down.

In the sky's sensual pout, the crazy kindness
Of statues, the scraps of leaves still blowing around
Self-importantly after winter was well under way;
In the closed greeting, the firm handclasp,
Was matter enough for one or more dreams,
Even bad ones, but certainly some getting grim
Around the edges. We smile at these,

Thinking them matter for a child's euphuistic
Tale of what goes on in the morning,
After everyone but the cat has left. But can you
See otherwise? O ecstatic
Receiver of what's there to be received,
How we belabor thee, how much better
To wait and to prepare our waiting
For the grand rush, the mass of detail
Still compacted in the excitement that lies ahead,
Like a Japanese paper flower.

The Big Cloud

For ages man has labored to put his dreams in order. Look at the result.
Once an idea like the correct time is elucidated
It must fade or spread. Decay, under the old tree, is noted.
That's why we frame them, try to keep them on a wall,
Though it is decreed that the companionable
Trooping down to be with us, to partly become us
Must continue for they and we to flourish:
The obliging feathers once parted,
The object of our sight, grass, just sits there
Like an empty flowerpot on a windowsill.

And a new dream gets us involved further
In that closeness. Yes, I knew there
Were sheets of tulips and pointed leaves
To screen us from each other, what we were all about,
And an announcement made against the lukewarm atmosphere of the room
To all that did or did not belong in it.

Finally, it seems, they have scattered.
Not one specimen was actually available.
And they call this peace, living our lives, and so on.
To point the finger of blame—ah, surely, at no one?
Each system trickles out into its set number of instances.
Poles strike bottom,
Finding the river sludge good to them, a companionable feeling.
Meetings occur under grotesquely overscaled arcades,
Last words are uttered, and first love
Ascends to its truly majestic position unimpaired.

Letters were strewn across the floor,
Singing the joyful song of how no one was ever going to read them.
Trees and wisteria rose and sank in the breeze,
And laughter danced in the dim fields beyond the schoolhouse:
It was existence again in all its tautness,
Playing its adolescent joke, its pictures

Teasing our notion of fragility with their monumental permanence.
But life was never the same again. Something faltered,
Something went away.

Not a First

It's one of those days I guess—
All my talking is like a novel that has to be opened.
Then angels appear
In old clothes, speaking the roar
We were all taught long ago.
Yet a whisper circumvents this. One just walks away.
The season is stalled
And no one really knows where the next one will be.

It is not an honest façade.
The streets are perfectly ruled
But the light has gone out of them. To have a good time
One must imagine an otherness so dour
It silences one. Then,
Out of a shrub perhaps, the voice turns interested again,
Plans are made, destinations reached
At the time printed in the schedule,
And life is perceived again as something that never paused,
Was there in the fir branches when the wind stooped,
Painless and aglow, its fever
A thing now of an imagination
Increasingly distracted by the glitter
Of small lights on the wet pavement; the "Yes,
This is what we came for, but where
Have they put those others? Their drab shoes,
The way they smile and whine?
Wasn't it true then
That life is a novel or an opera,
That there is no third place?"

You need only rough outlines. The mitred corners
Are chamfered now, and the sky is awash
With light like soap. In vacant lots
The life is tapered to fit. No allowance was made
For citrus groves on the old plan of the city.

It's all torn apart now, in any case,
But our loves and their regions
Stay on, permeated with their obsolescence,
A warming voice in the car.

Polite Distortions

Already the conning tower is issuing conflicting bulletins:
"Profligate is profligate" (or so one would like to hear it
Into the silence of inertia), but what chiefly arrests one,
What one is chiefly led to contemplate, isn't that sensible
If fragmented discourse, but how, with no children around
To contest it, the same old story is different
With each new telling. The steps, slanted to be sure,
Lead to a warmer place where there is nothing to notice
Or everything to escape notice. We linger against a pattern
Of hills with tractor obbligato, and everything comes
To sway in our sense (well, with it). One is released
From the clothes of day, one by one; an invisible valet
Takes each one away, never to be seen again. Oh well, we
Were meant to rest at this point so that the laundry
Of our thinking will be spread out on bushes and not
Come to tempt us too much with the long shadows of causality
Striking deep into its expansionist mass to let the bare
Branches form a tentative yet definitive icing or hairnet over its
Accidented terrain. That's how determinism does it:
Jack fell down and broke his crown,
And Jill came tumbling after.

The sensible thing is to review, always to review.
In this way new steps are seen to have been already
Invented, while others, old, premature ones may be
Returning to interact with them in a cone of distance
Drawing ever tighter around wrists, throats. Profligate isn't
Anymore, I'll betcha, I'll just betcha, but who can
Know in the violet flood of embarrassment or pure
Terror, put off, put on again. They tell us there is so much to say
And they operate on this principle, but once we have gone away
Others will take over and not care to speak much about it.
Too bad. Whatever waywardness there was was our
Fault but now there isn't too much to say about it.
It's like the grass at the end of March, still brown, not quite green.

Fourth Prize

Only the desire to get lost in everything—
Only the opal ovals of the drive
Until the crash of this afternoon, late
Anxiety and avarice until everything settles
Again and for the millionth time the wish
Is forgotten. The sapling thrashes in the no wind
Of the street lamp, desperate. Good citizens almost
Have retired. Wind up the chain, beware
The knots: if you can use any of this, do so,
But the fond and the tired are long in bed.

Try it here, maybe it can help here
Too, but get out of the house in case
Of a delay, no matter how fortunate. Or
Parade in the streets, it's shameless, it's
Not shameless, OK. Are these
Not petals falling on our heads, so slowly?
Isn't that your son's tibia in the pilaf?
How many old cars were stalled, pretending
To be stopped for a red light, that this was
A parade of them from someplace to someone's place?
And the thrill one was supposed to win
But it was only announced in the newspaper
And never came back? How about it?

And as I lie shut in this long coffin
Of an apartment, thinking of the damp,
And some squib of light tries to protect me
(From my own none-too-intense convictions?
Please: sail with it, make sure
You are with it and out of its way
Until such time as the execution, the wreath
Of ink comes, and then talk baby talk
From the summit of the high-rise; don't
Look down, falling is out of the question)

And the congruent shores gracefully join
Toes, and armpits, so that this smiling
Land is the result: it appears, sun under vines, long
Straight looks into the wilderness.

And what has become clear becomes clear for so very long.
Burnished cherries were meant for these hidden moments
Of respite and of rage, not moments for our times, though,
Remember. I don't know, it's all too comically abstract
Yet it fits in with what isn't until a kind of
Bathrobe of the age is stitched together, patched together,
Ready to ensure in principle the kind of moment we had
When young, to undo the colored past and extract
Whatever good may come of it now, at this late date, really
When one has become a little oversimplified and therefore anxious.

Some Money

I said I am awkward.
I said we make fools of our lives
For a little money and a coat.
The great tree, once grown, passes over.
I said you can catch all kinds of weird activities.

Meanwhile the child disturbs you.
You are never asked back with its dog
And the fishing pole leans against the steps.
Why have all the windows darkened?
The laurel burned its image into the sky like smoke?

All was gold and shiny in the queen's parlor.
In the pigsty outside it was winter however
With one headache after another
Leading to the blasted bush
On which a felt hat was stuck
Closer to the image of you, of how it feels.
The dogs were in time for no luck.
The lobster shouted how it was long ago
No pen mightier than this said the object
As though to ward off a step
To kiss my sweetheart in the narrow alley
Before it was wartime and the cold ended
On that note.

Winter Weather Advisory

What have we proved? That we don't have the one idea
Worth having, that all else is beneath us,
If within our grasp? But no, it should be in some book
Perhaps, the book one has never read: there it keeps
Its high literacy like a pearl: no point in displaying it,
It's too eloquent, too gracious, for these times
At least. So it's a question of "these times,"
Now and forever. If a dog goes on barking
For more than twenty minutes, if the last page
Of the newspaper is never reached due to the cataclysmic
Interruptions, it must be something about us
And the way we handle this skein of time
We are just getting to know, and the pendulum shatters
All of it into mutually combative fragments, some bad,
Some worth entertaining, but the complex,
Much too complex, some would say, aviary-as-environment
That results is the piece of real estate one inherited long ago,
That partially submerged orange grove in Florida. In this way
The categories are paraded as one, one falls out dumbly
To join the general direction at the appointed time.

Chief among them was cleverness: how much stomach
One had for the "merely clever"; besides, what is "merely"
In that sense? A looking up to something, something too humane
To be in the way, yet too central
To be ignored? That is about the last thing importance
Had in mind for us all along, that accident, watershed,
Or gathering of the tribes in the name of sophistication
Perhaps, or whatever results when loneliness is split.

And I am afraid it will mean mostly weather
From here on in, a climate too hungry to become
The protagonist, leaving one to sit and chafe at not
Having memorized one's speech perfectly, and in the end
This becomes a number, a turn. Of course it was

Perhaps built on spec, someone commissioned it
Probably, but here and now it is our sole contribution
To the success of the soiree. I think, I look
At these hands like wild swans flying: when
Will they come back, on what day, and will I know the truth
Then, and so be able to accept them as mere painted
Portents of what each of us wants to know, from the most
Hardened criminal to the chance embodiment of purest
Innocence, some bore from off the street? And if the sale
Continues and the dark, squishy footprints in the slush
Take over our notion of a country as a map would, can I
In the August of office buildings and air conditioning petition
Not a retrial but a restaging of the games as they
Would in all probability have ended? Will the truth leak out
And, if so, will there have been any advantage to proving
Over and over again that it wasn't worth doing
And we did it to please our neighbors and the little girl
With the hoop? The page falls just so
This time, all the cleverness worked out of its system,
Backed into a generally accepted notion of what history consists of.
We ride and ride, and still the view comes on.

Never to Get It Really Right

A tan light stalks the rooms now
(With their neoclassic moldings, waiting
For the tedium of words to subside),
That suits it all by draining the life out of it
All. She says, I was inert, I still am.
I think my touch carries almost to your mouth
A beaker of living silence
But then I have to excuse myself.
I am gone. I am always down here, gone
In the wet and wishing vectors of the street
That builds such an uproar. Noises run over me.
Do you know my name? I won't be gone long,
Nor stay long once I'm back, you can bet.

In the morning there were thousands of mermaids
Expecting orders, but the once-weary enchanter
Kept them at bay, and nothing was performed that day,
Whether from civic malice, indifference, or just forgetting
For a few moments some thing that should never be forgotten
And being stuck with the different colors everything
Was as a result—not the chief one either—
Of it. The chauffeur lays his plan on the seat,
It being lunchtime. And beautiful birds, like bengalis
But more dazzlingly tinted, hesitate above cars.
An elevator shoots up eighty stories with some debris in it:
"Sorry, this wasn't meant for you." Well I mean
We all of us like a little remembrance at times
But the absence thereof won't make crops shrivel.
Besides, the gold of winter is clanging already
In dusty hallways. I have my notebook ready.
And the richly falling light will transform us
Then, into mute and privileged spectators.
I never do know how to end any season,
Do you? And it never matters; between the catch
And the fall, a new series has been propounded

With brio and élan. Looks like the face powder
On things is the next stage, step
In the staircase that plummets us from there
To here, without connivance or turpitude
On our part, and leaves us
Where it counts: just bemused revelers, no
Qualms, no frustrations, not even a sense of its being new.

An even sparkle contains us.
We are only fabulous beasts, after all.

Gorboduc

Well, I graduated, so you'll have to.
This is the way the annoyance of the world is divided:
No leisure, except on Sundays, and no time for thought during the week.
In summer we all go away and hide somewhere
But are back by September, ready to think about new problems,
Tackle the infinite, basing our stratagem
On knowledge of one inch of it. But then the story blows away,
And what can you do, howling without a script?

One could try to remember the purpose of knot gardens—
Perhaps a way to fold oneself
Into the symmetry of nature
Without coming away looking like a foolish old man?

Yet so many riders are here and there,
Children who give up all knowledge
At the first brush with the wicked fairy who wants only to make us cry.
Striding from one mood to the next
Is the worst, likely to involve you in more changes
Than were called for originally, especially the big one
Of standing in place—what is there to get out of it?
Realization someday that nothing is too permanent
And fickleness can't be counted on either?
Luckily clothes stabilize this a little:
I am wearing my morning shirt; the jacket
Slips easily off my shoulders when evening arrives.
Things tie us to the tide
As it progresses easily, for miles along the shore, and in the end
Its largely ceremonial relation to that entity
Is shuttered, put away
With the time it contracted for
And that is now so late,
Dwindled to a single eighth-note of a bird,
To a polished, square leaf.

These two guys in the front yard—
Are they here to help? It's true I sent for someone
Years ago, but so much has come unbuilt
Since then, so many columns of figures
Left to fall apart in the weather, as it normally freezes
And rots things, that I am not sure if all this is worth doing,
If any of it ever was. I can hear a clarinet
Sounding clear notes of heaven
And am taller to enjoy, to disburden myself
Of all that got lost in the telling:
Prismatic shapes of day
As it came in and shook us, its average grace
Rounded off by nice easy stories
And the procession of effulgent numerals
Happily buried in earth
That won't teach us anything.

The Romantic Entanglement

Ah, you don't know what fun it is
Arriving in the rain just as night has changed the subject
To a downhill story of professors, pigs and pianos,
To the sermon of the moment.
How the lamplight crackled then! It was like the elision
Of a final vowel, and also a new adventure, proposed on a pinnacle
Not previously noted.

And snaking along a steep shelf of brushwood
To be close to a river, parallel: the fun of that too.

In dreams when you ask me
What kind of time we're having and
I reply something about emerald moss
Coating the standpipes of this century,
It all turns in on us,
Focuses on us,
Is us finally, no beauty left
In the eye of the beholder, only mistaken
Beginnings, false notes, marches, tunes, arias
With so little to recommend them.
But you saw only mussel gatherers
Waist-deep offshore,
Forcing an ever-diminishing sustenance
From the sea's floor.

And we can see now how it's impossible
To answer anything and stay unnatural,
Response being, by its very nature, romantic,
The very urge to romanticism. The precise itch.
What if I met you at the store
Five seconds from now—would the sleepers still elide their snores,
Would the stares of the salespeople compensate us
For what we shoplifted,
Cold as ashes in a grate after we're home?

Wet Are the Boards

Not liking what life has in it,
"It's probably dead, whatever it is,"
You said, and turned, and thought
Of one spot on the ground, what it means to all of us
Passing through the earth. And the reasonable, filleted
Nymph of the fashions of the air points to that too:
"No need to be deprived. We are all
Friends here,
And whatever it takes to get us out of the mess we're in
One of us has."

Fair enough, and the spirited bulk,
The work of a local architect, knows how to detach itself
From the little puffs issuing from the mouths of the four winds,
Yet not too much, and be honest
While still remaining noble and sedate.
The tepees on the front lawn
Of the governor's palace become a fixture there
And were cast in stone after the originals rotted away.
Fish tanks glinted from within the varnished
Halls of jurisprudence and it was possible to save
The friezes, of Merovingian thrust,
And so much else made to please the senses:
Like a plum tree dripping brilliants
On a round dirt bed, and all the stories of the ducks.
Now if only I were a noncombatant—
Which brings us back to the others: philosophers,
Pedants, and criminals intent on enjoying the public view—
Is it just another panorama?
For we none of us
Can determine strictly what they are thinking,
Even the one we walk arm in arm with
Through the darkling purple air of spring, so when it comes
Time to depart our good-byes will read automatically true or false
According to what has gone before.

And that loneliness will accompany us
On the far side of parting, when what we dream, we read.
No hand is outstretched
Through the bored gloom unless more thinking wants to take us elsewhere
Into space that seems changed, by luck or just by time hanging around,
And the mystery of the family that bore you
Into the race that is, reversing the story

So that the end showed through the paper as the beginning
And all children were nice again.
Pause again at the scenery
Whirling to destroy itself, and what a different face
It wears when order smiles, as I think it
Does here. Our costumes
Must never be folded and put back into the trunk again,
Or someone too young for the part is going to step up
And say, "Listen, I made it. It's mine,"
In a November twilight when the frost is creeping over you
As surely as waves across a beach, since no chill is complete
Without our unique participation. And when you walk away
You might reflect that this is an aspect
In which all of the cores and seeds are visible,
That it's a matter of not choosing to see.

And Some Were Playing Cards,
and Some Were Playing Dice

And there you have it. I can't overpraise your response
Though I can clock it by its choked glimmer,
Like a night sound for which there is no explanation.

And I can see farther out of the situation of you and me
By the wan halo it insistently projects.
I am here. There is no such person as you,
Yet you are funny, and silly, and in your voice there are
Abrupt meanders and chambers so casual I cannot
Think of listening any longer. Deaf, you understand too much
And absolutely do not want this knowledge
Though to people on earth it looks like a circus in the sky
And the weather that depends on it is talked about for days.

Fall Pageant

I.

From this valley they say you are leaving.
Remember to tie your shoes. From these hectares,
The relations among the undefined emptinesses of the sky,
Gathered at the top. From abject birds.

Still, a light wash of gray is on things,
A scumbling. It said these places were new
Just last year
And still are, in places. Yet there is nowhere
To hide this year, and the newness
Keeps coming on. No one explained to it. Is encroaching.

II.

I thought I never heard before in my life
Such canyons of notes, abundant trills,
Immortal fortissimi. I could give it all up
For a chauffeur's life, but daren't scratch
The newness lest a new complaint be issued,
Stone demerits. One wakes up parched,
Glad to be back in the land of sunrises,
But your son who has a gun says you can't go back there.

All around us, too distant for company,
New towers are on the march.
We are experiencing audio difficulties.
Yet there was a time when this was sweet
And she came to me crying, saving the best pieces
For the end and upset me with her tears,
Rolled me over and I was all right again.
Gee, thanks. People are so much kinder
When one is old, but so little kind as well

Since the cracks are big enough for more things to fall through.
Afternoon wanes obstinately.

And we three are on the floor:
Tell me do you like it here
This land of no ships and signs pointed into the wind?
Of briar patch and gorilla, salesman and aerosol,
Thing eked out with thing. And in the beginning
So many free gifts were promised, we thought we'd have a major one
By evening and recoup some of our losses:
No chance. Here, portals are open.
Fire penetrates the very memory
Of what we were going to do today, of dishes
And the elect. The toy that was never
Taken out of its box. The sun rushes in,
Washes the baseboard and is gone, briefly.
Another moment has taken over.
And for that we should keep the covenant.
Never to worry when the cannon are locked in place,
The woods filled with self-congratulatory messages.
The fire trenches deep and alight.

For one messenger is sure to pull up
In front of the house next day with a corrective
To last night's blocus, and there are bound to be hallowed stones on
    the floor.

Or it could be sweetly idyllic, experience not needed
And still get blamed for getting lost on the way, that hotel
We saw. Its clink of coin ringing
Neither true nor falsely true: an errand boy of a thing.

And we circulate:
Meat of autumn in the air of the corridor.

III.

I stepped out of the saturation of your garment
For a moment, for a reason. Only to plunge back in
A little later, when the closet was different.
You don't keep me at bay or away.

There is everything I can say to you.
Your voice is a rapturous clarinet
That doesn't listen, ripe, evenings.
You tell me to go away, and I stay.

I know where I'm going.
And I know who's going with me.
And the fear of shattering at the top
Is hearsay of leaves wiped away
Inside a grotto. I purposely withheld the name
And you guessed it; you have already read my thoughts
By the time I have them.

I can't even be wistful and get away with it.
Otherwise any type of posturing will do,
At the very basement of the maelstrom
Where looks get exchanged, hands touched.

And the problem of youth in our society
Looks fetchingly away.
Throw something over me
It seems to say.

In all wet, lost voices it turns out this year
To have been fruition, and advantage. Next season
The rules will have been deconstructed, and so much
That is old or simply extra will be preserved
That the shape will no longer be the point, nor

The formlessness. The monument
Didn't work out as planned, but we have been taken in
And as it were anointed by a band of robbers
Who even let us visit home sometimes
Provided we swear on our honor to return
And not tell anyone about it. So, although
It's a little damp here, it suits me fine
Since I have so much to think over, and, even worse,
Write a report on, like the rondel or villanelle it is.

One Coat of Paint

We will all have to just hang on for a while,
It seems, now. This could mean "early retirement"
For some, if only for an afternoon of pottering around
Buying shoelaces and the like. Or it could mean a spell
In some enchanter's cave, after several centuries of which
You wake up curiously refreshed, eager to get back
To the crossword puzzle, only no one knows your name
Or who you are, really, or cares much either. To seduce
A fact into becoming an object, a pleasing one, with some
Kind of esthetic quality, which would also add to the store
Of knowledge and even extend through several strata
Of history, like a pin through a cracked wrist bone,
Connecting these in such a dynamic way that one would be forced
To acknowledge a new kind of superiority without which the world
Could no longer conduct its business, even simple stuff like bringing
Water home from wells, coals to hearths, would of course be
An optimal form of it but in any case the thing's got to
Come into being, something has to happen, or all
We'll have left is disagreements, *désagréments,* to name a few.
O don't you see how necessary it is to be around,
To be ferried from here to that near, smiling shore
And back again into the arms of those that love us,
Not many, but of such infinite, superior sweetness
That their lie is for us and it becomes stained, encrusted,
Finally gilded in some exasperating way that turns it
To a truth plus something, delicate and dismal as a star,
Cautious as a drop of milk, so that they let us
Get away with it, some do at any rate?

Offshore Breeze

Perhaps I have merely forgotten,
Perhaps it really was like you say.
How can I know?
While life grows increasingly mysterious and dangerous
With nobody else really visible,
And I am alone and quiet
Like the grass this day of no wind
And sizzling knowledge.
The leaves fall, fall off and burn.

At least one can nap until the Day of Judgment—
Or can one? Be careful what you say, the perturbed
Flock shifts and retreats
In a colorful equation of long standing.
No one knew what microorganisms
Were metamorphosing. I like you
Because it's all I *can* do.

What happens is you get the unreconstructed story,
An offshore breeze pushing one gently away,
Not far away. And the leggings of those meeting to
See about it are a sunset,
Brilliant and disordered, and sharp
As a word held in the mouth too long.
And he spat out the pit.

Savage Menace

The castle was infested with rats;
For weeks no one had unpacked the laundry
Or dusted the rungs of the chairs.
"Your voice sounds near. Try to find
A door that will lead to us."

Sun's shadow, enormous guessing.

Or water streaming off stones, shallowness
Where one might wade alone, miracle
That happens too seldom for us in such times
As these were. The madhouse and the saloon
Crumbled, and on such occasions manners
Are jettisoned too and no one cares
What anyone thinks. The budget is ignored.

No one wants to stay in the house though outside
It's not exactly what one had in mind either:
Small groups do wander and conversations
Are initiated. It would be rash to say
Too much though. And a sudden shower
Cancels it, rafts of sunlight and cloud
Slant dangerously, tipping the load
Into other rubbish and there is no last word.

Benign at times the weather takes on
An increasingly noticeable edge
As it shambles deeper into autumn
To the flat promise of winter.
Balls of trees, yet everything
Has been thoroughly harvested; the gleaners
Return home empty-handed as night invests the fields.

A small farmer devastated by enclosure,
Plummeted into ruin, must question the sincere

Anxiety of clouds and fields once everything
Is taken over and all the morsels have been distributed
At last. Quickly, the storm bent
To extinguish one's anxiety
About not having a place to hide,
And it was all up to us. No more roasted pheasants,
Figs and grapes cascading from golden
Cornucopias, songs about uncompromising
Nebuchadnezzar finding it difficult to reestablish contact
With the court and so on.

Or if a few dandelions
Came up or there was an abundance
Of powder strewing the Canadian lakes there was
Still no time to get offshore:
The limpid trellis of bird notes merely
Underscored this and kept the vote

From turning out.
Now, most windows are opaque
And though the sun breathes there is little
Cause for rejoicing except in the locked,
Silent chamber of midnight:
It is there one goes to hear the riot act
Read aloud and perhaps to fall asleep
Fitfully, before day arrives
With another list of patrons and donors
To be assimilated, to be ignored.

And though you and I can never catch up with
Everything thoughtful that happens
To us, we are bold to say:
I like it. This is, after all, why I came here.
If everybody was twins we'd be
No doubt happier but all in all it has

Only to be mentioned in the bibliography
For one person to go on caring
About what happens to him or her,
To be as a child when the baker's truck
Arrives and somehow fracture a sequence
Out of these long trails of figures like collapsed
Bean vines in the precious dust
That salutes us with yet another color.

The Leopard and the Lemur

The voice is stilled, that once
Spoke out of a crack in the wall:
The origins of the earth are eroded;
We don't know at what point history begins
And the speech of the sky is clouded.
But if it please the god to turn back,
To turn around, the gap would be invisibly
Paved over and foreign accounts perhaps
Opened, a shuffling commerce begin
In what has been a dry stream bed until now.
May lions begin to pace and so wrench us
Back from the ill-humored precipice
Into a dream of today as found:
No jewels only a piece of blue
Above the rue Taylor and dried money
In the laundry and you all return
For your lesson and there is no school today,
Only a few imperfect, timeless moments
To tease the vanished splendor again
Until we swim free and later remember
Stray hours and in that time learn something.

Yet: the days are messy, believe
Not everything will come to pass
That was achieved and heights promised
Are dummy until now, and then depressions
For a long time after that, until echolalia
Unlocks trapped springs, blossoms in the gush
Of multiple and staggered misunderstandings.
Then with a broad brush a single tree
On a low rise is ushered into being,
Asked if it intends to stay
Like this, a reproach to solitary
Coachmen on their platforms under a horned moon.
And this, and this shall happen, at first

Not pointedly, but shall gradually come to take your place
As more grow up and decide and still more
Find themselves forgotten, yet strangely
Familiar and correct in the mirror, the time
God took to tell them about it and withdraw:
Leopard to himself, a confusion of many identities
To all others. Let the old man dream
Awhile. Tonight nobody is going anywhere.

By the Flooded Canal

Which custard? The dish of not-so-clean snow
Or the sherry trifle with bloodlike jam and riotous
Yellow stuff running down the steep sides
Into ambiguity, an ambiguous thing. Do you want me
To come here anymore.

Then I met your father.
I hadn't written anything for almost a year.

Unfortunately he wasn't very attractive.

He married a woman with the curious name of Lael.
It all took me by surprise, coming up behind me
Like a book. As I stand and look at it now.
Then all the thoughts went out of my head,
Running away into the wind. I didn't have *him*
To think about anymore, I didn't have myself either.
It was all notes for a book that has been written, that nobody
Is ever going to read. A bottle with a note in it
Washes up on shore and no one sees it, no one picks it up.

And then one day it was windy
With fog, and I hate the combination of fog and wind,
Besides being too cool for what it looked like. The sun
Was probably out just a short distance above our heads.
Not a good drying day. And I hung the laundry out
On the clothesline, all black and white
And the news got lost somewhere inside. My news.

Do you come here any longer with the intention of killing
Something, no you have nothing in mind.
And I shift, arranging the pieces
In a cardboard drawer. No two are alike, and I like that.

The kitten on the stairs heard it
Once, in disbelief, and I go

To sales, and buy only what we need.
The old men are a strong team.

And I mix it up with them, it's quite like
Having encounters if one is a poplar
In a row of them and so involved
With one's reflection as well as one's two neighbors only I say
I didn't mean for it to be this way
But since it has happened I'm glad and will continue to work,
To strive for your success. I don't expect thanks
And am happy in the small role assigned me,
Really. I think I'll go out in the garage.

Bilking the Statues

If I come to you empty-handed, thaumaturge-like,
It is so you can see my arms are wide open,
Bereft of you, that in the sunshine we can play
And return to separate dreams later, in the night
Of the car. And all that we do within and to

Each other be kept distinct from evening's dazzle,
From the colorful drowned insects in the grass,
And my name be invisibly scratched on everything.
You were never like a lighthouse, or even a buoy,
But more like the vacant port itself

After most of the longshoremen had been laid off.
And if some things still divert you, such as the point
Of the cold this winter, attentiveness had laid it
On so thick we shall never get our speeches right:
Not in what remains of this century, at least,

Or even the dividend of any ripe, unhappening time.
Regret frosts over the numerals in their glass case
And it is of a very valuable, ancient kind,
Bringing its own opera glasses and children along
For the ride, for protection. To get clear of any of this

Requires a push of such magnitude that one can only
Awake far from a dream that hasn't even scrolled its signature
Breath on what happened to the sleep that pillowed it
Like velvet. Too many things shroud us from having
To realize one is not awake, yet these steps are real,

And the road winds uphill all the way, *yes*
To the very end. It sounds like tripe when you feel,
Let alone say, it, but the good intentions were good,
Paving the way admirably for thin lines of painted
Soldiers to "evolve" on. And this week all that waves to

It is trash, shop after shuttered shop lining the
Winding, narrow street. Someday we may play guessing
Games but now is what's right for our country, our stars
And us. Notice we're near a tank farm. And cousins
Arrive from all over the country, furled sails are breathing

Even as they hug the masts more tightly. In short, everyone
Is waiting for the booked speaker, but only things
Can voice these sentiments now, as in "I don't much appreciate
That towel," or trial. He's not much, just a kangaroo,
Just six feet of kangaroo. But we ought to go over

The books, or the top, just to verify they left out something.
I didn't. I don't know the people here anymore,
Only the children I used to know, long ago, when earth
And sky were young, and even then something had been left
Or let out, as witnessed by the fact that no one ever came to see us,

Yet the postman groaned and swore under a voluminous pack
Of correspondence, coming up the walk each day. And how
Were we supposed to know, it being dusk, the ashen
Boys, the trilogy of them hanging around that way to covet
And comfort us while somebody in a velveteen coat was

Up ahead there, intentions scattered on the water?
We knit these beginnings like brows, and the only
One who ever comes to inquire about it is the elderly
Janitor, long deceased. It seems there was a table spread,
And then, and them? Yet one was pleased to see even

That much, it wasn't as though flamingos had begun announcing
It. Besides they're just statues one can take along,
If one wants. And the garden, why the garden
Was delighted with everything, though the times were not
All that good, and even night might well turn out to be eternal.

The Ice Storm

isn't really a storm of course because unlike most storms it isn't one till it's over and people go outside and say will you look at that. And by then it's of course starting to collapse. Diamond rubble, all galled glitter, heaps of this and that in corners and beside posts where the draft has left them—are you sure it's this you were waiting for while the storm—the real one—pressed it all into the earth to emphasize a point that melts away as fast as another idea enters the chain of them in the conversation about earth and sky and woods and how you should be good to your parents and not cheat at cards. The summer's almost over it seems to say. Did I say summer I meant to say winter it seems to say. You know when nature really has to claw like this to get her effects that something's not ripe or nice, i.e., the winter, our favorite of the seasons, the one that goes by quickest although you almost never hear anyone say, I wonder where the winter has gone. But anyone engaged in the business of swapping purity for depth will understand what I mean. So we all eyeball it, agog, for a while. And soon our attention is trapped by news from the cities, by what comes over the wireless—*heated,* and alight. How natural then to retreat into what we have been doing, trying to capture the old songs, the idiot games whose rules have been forgotten. "Here we go looby, looby." And the exact name of the season that stings like a needle made of frozen mercury falls through the infinitesimal hole in our consciousness, to plummet hundreds of leagues into the sea and vanish in a perpetual descent toward the ocean floor, whatever and wherever that may be, and the great undersea storms and cataclysms will leave no trace on the seismographs each of us wears in the guise of a head.

To do that, though—get up and out from under the pile of required reading such as obituary notices of the near-great—"He first gained employment as a schoolmaster in his native Northamptonshire. Of his legendary wit, no trace remains"—is something that will go unthought of until another day. Sure we know that the government and the president want it. But we know just as surely that until the actual slippage occurs, the actual moment of uncertainty by two or more of the plates or tectons that comprise the earth's crust, nobody is ever going to be moved to the point of action. You might as well call it a night, go to sleep under a bushel basket. For the probability of that moment occurring is next to nil. I mean it will probably never happen and if it does, chances are we won't be around to witness any of it.

The warp, the woof. (What, actually, are they? Never mind, save that for another time when the old guy's gotten a bit more soused). Or the actual strings of words on the two pages of a book, like "I was reading this novel, I think the author was associated with the Kailyard School." What's that? Wait, though—I think I know. What I really want to know is how will this affect me, make me better in the future? Maybe make me a better conversationalist? But nobody I know ever talks about the Kailyard School, at least not at the dinner parties I go to. What, then? Will it be that having accomplished the tale of this reading there will only be about seven million more books to go, and that's something, or is it more the act of reading something, of being communicated to by an author and thus having one's ideas displaced like the water that pebbles placed by the stork's beak slowly force out of the beaker—*beaker?* do you suppose? No, I wasn't suggesting anything like that. I want to cut out of this conversation or discourse. Why? Because it doesn't seem to be leading anywhere. Besides it could compromise me when the results become known, and by results I mean the slightest ripple that occurs as when the breeze lifts a corner of the vast torpid flag drooping at its standard, like the hairline crack in the milk-white china of the sky, that indicates something is off, something less likable than the situation a few moments before has assumed its place in the preordained hierarchy of things. Something like the leaves of this plant with their veins that almost look parallel though they are radiating from their centers of course.

It's odd about things like plants. Today I found a rose in full bloom in the wreck of the garden, all the living color and sentience but also the sententiousness drained out of it. What remained was like a small flower in the woods, too pale and sickly to notice. No, sickly isn't the right word, the thing was normal and healthy by its own standards, and thriving merrily along its allotted path toward death. Only we hold it up to some real and abject notion of what a living organism ought to be and paint it as a scarecrow that frightens birds away (presumably) but isn't able to frighten itself away. Oh, no, it's far too clever for that! But our flower, the one we saw, really had no need of us to justify its blooming where it did. So we ought to think about our own position on the path. Will it ever be anything more than that of pebble? I wonder. And they scratch, some of them feverishly, at whatever meaning it might be supposed to yield up, of course expiring as it does so. But our rose gains its distinction just by being stuck there as though by the distracted hand of a caterer putting the finishing touch on some grand floral display for a society wedding that will be over in a few minutes, a season not of its own naming. Why appear at a time when the idea of a flower can make no sense, not even in its isolation? It's just that nature forces us into odd positions and then sits back to hear us squawk but may, indeed, derive no comfort or pleasure from this. And as I lifted it gently I saw that it was doing what it was supposed to do—miming freshness tracked by pathos. What more do you want? it seemed to say. Leave me in this desert . . .

As I straightened my footsteps to accommodate the narrow path that has been chosen for me I begin to cringe at the notion that I can never be assimilated here, no, not like the rose blooming grotesquely out of season even, but must always consider the sharp edges of the slender stones set upright in the earth, to be my guide and commentator, on this path. I was talking to some of the others about it. But if it didn't matter then, it matters now, now that I begin to get my bearings in this gloom and see how I could improve on the distraught situation all around me, in the darkness and tarnished earth. Yet who will save me from myself if they can't? I can't, certainly, yet I tell myself it all seems like fun and will work out in the end. I expect I will be asked a question I can answer and then be handed a big prize. They're working on it.

So the sunlit snow slips daintily down the waterway to the open sea, the car with its driver along the looping drives that bisect suburbs and then flatten out through towns that are partly rural though with some suburban characteristics. Only I stay here alone, waiting for it to reach the point of cohesion. Or maybe I'm not alone, maybe there are other me's, but in that case the cohesion may have happened already and we are no wiser for it, despite being positioned around to comment on it like statues around a view. The dry illumination that results from that will not help us, it will always be as though we had never happened, ornaments on a structure whose mass remains invisible or illegible.

October 28. Three more days till November. I expect this to happen in a soft explosion of powdery light, dull and nameless, though not without a sense of humor in its crevices, where darkness still lives and enjoys going about its business. There are too many stones to make it interesting to hobble from one to another. Perhaps in a few days ... Maybe by the time I finish the course I am taking, if sirens don't dislodge me from this pure and valid niche. I feel that this season is being pulled over my head like a dress, difficult to spot the dirt in its mauve and brick traceries. I am being taken out into the country. Trees flash past. All is perhaps for the best then since I am going, and they are going with us, with us as we go. The past is only a pond. The present is a lake of grass. Between your two futures, yours and his, numbing twigs chart the pattern of lifeless chatter in shut-down night, starstruck the magnitudes that would make us theirs, too cold to matter to themselves, let us be off anywhere, to Alaska, to Arizona. I am fishing for compliments. The afternoon lasts forever.

April Galleons

Something *was* burning. And besides,
At the far end of the room a discredited waltz
Was alive and reciting tales of the conquerors
And their lilies—is all of life thus
A tepid housewarming? And where do the scraps
Of meaning come from? Obviously,
It was time to be off, in another
Direction, toward marshlands and cold, scrolled
Names of cities that sounded as though they existed,
But never had. I could see the scow
Like a nail file pointed at the pleasures
Of the great open sea, that it would stop for me,
That you and I should sample the disjointedness
Of a far-from-level deck, and then return, some day,
Through the torn orange veils of an early evening
That will know our names only in a different
Pronunciation, and then, and only then,
Might the profit-taking of spring arrive
In due course, as one says, with the gesture
Of a bird taking off for some presumably
Better location, though not major, perhaps,
In the sense that a winged guitar would be major
If we had one. And all trees seemed to exist.

Then there was a shorter day with dank
Tapestries streaming initials of all the previous owners
To warn us into silence and waiting. Would the mouse
Know us now, and if so, how far would propinquity
Admit discussion of the difference: crumb or other
Less perceptible boon? It was all going
To be scattered anyway, as far from one's wish
As the root of the tree from the center of the earth
From which it nonetheless issued in time to
Inform us of happy blossoms and tomorrow's
Festival of the vines. Just being under them

Sometimes makes you wonder how much you know
And then you wake up and you know, but not
How much. In intervals in the twilight notes from an
Untuned mandolin seem to co-exist with their
Question and the no less urgent reply. Come
To look at us but not too near or its familiarity
Will vanish in a thunderclap and the beggar-girl,
String-haired and incomprehensibly weeping, will
Be all that is left of the golden age, our
Golden age, and no longer will the swarms
Issue forth at dawn to return in a rain of mild
Powder at night removing us from our boring and
Unsatisfactory honesty with tales of colored cities,
Of how the mist built there, and what were the
Directions the lepers were taking
To avoid these eyes, the old eyes of love.

Grateful acknowledgment is made to the following publications, in which some of the poems in this book first appeared: *Boulevard*: "Bilking the Statues"; *Conjunctions*: "Finnish Rhapsody"; *The New Yorker*: "Wet Are the Boards," "The Romantic Entanglement," "Vetiver," "Alone in the Lumber Business," "Vaucanson," "April Galleons," "Frost," and "Sighs and Inhibitions"; *The New York Review of Books*: "A Mood of Quiet Beauty" and "Never to Get It Really Right"; *Numbers*: "Song: 'Mostly Places...'"; *Poetry*: "Unreleased Movie," "Morning Jitters," "Adam Snow," "Ostensibly," "Riddle Me," and "Amid Mounting Evidence"; *PN Review*: "Forgotten Song" and "Railroad Bridge"; *Poetry Review*: "October at the Window" and "Disguised Zenith"; *Privates*: "Insane Decisions"; *riverrun*: "And Some Were Playing Cards, and Some Were Playing Dice"; *Shenandoah*: "One Coat of Paint"; *Scripsi*: "When half the time they don't know themselves..."; *Sulfur*: "Someone You Have Seen Before," "Dreams of Adulthood," and "Forgotten Sex"; *Temblor*: "The Ice Storm"; *Times Literary Supplement*: "By the Flooded Canal"; and *Verse*: "Posture of Unease."

"Not a First" was published in 1987 by Kaldewey Press as a book with drawings by Jonathan Lasker.

I wish to thank the John D. and Catherine T. MacArthur Foundation for a fellowship which was of great help in writing this book—J.A.